JUST A
LITTLE HOMEWORK

BY GINA AND MERCER MAYER

For Zeb,
For Ben,
For Arden,
For Jessie
The Homework-A-Trons

A GOLDEN BOOK • NEW YORK

Just a Little Homework book, characters, text, and images © 2004 Gina and Mercer Mayer. LITTLE CRITTER, MERCER MAYER'S LITTLE CRITTER, and MERCER MAYER'S LITTLE CRITTER and Logo are registered trademarks of Orchard House Licensing Company. All rights reserved under International and Pan-American Copyright Conventions. Published in the United States by Golden Books, an imprint of Random House Children's Books, a division of Random House, Inc., New York, and simultaneously in Canada by Random House of Canada Limited, Toronto. Golden Books, A Golden Book, and the G colophon are registered trademarks of Random House, Inc. Library of Congress Control Number: 2003107756
ISBN 0-375-82745-5
www.goldenbooks.com
Printed in the United States of America   First Edition 2004
1 0 9 8 7 6 5

Today when I got home from school, Mom asked if I had any homework. I said I had a little bit.

I went into the kitchen to make a snack. Mom said, "Let me see your homework sheet after your snack."

But I remembered I had left my
bike at the park. So I went to get it.

Some kids were playing tag,
so I joined in for just a minute.
I heard my mom calling me.
"Oops!" I said. "I gotta go."

I gave my mom my homework sheet.
She said, "You don't have very much homework. Why don't you do it right now, and then you can go out to play until dinnertime."

"Great idea, Mom," I answered.
I went to my room to do my homework.
But my hamster needed food and water.

Then I found my yo-yo, so I did a few tricks.
I hit my lamp doing the around-the-world.

Mom looked into my room and said, "What are you doing?"

"I knocked my lamp over by accident. I'll just clean it up."

"No," said Mom. "I will clean it up. You do your homework."

This homework was taking longer than
Mom thought, so I went into the den to do it
there. I turned on the TV for some company.

My favorite show was on. I thought
I would watch just a little bit.

Mom came in and turned off the TV and marched me into the kitchen. "Finish your homework first, then you can watch your show," she said.

That didn't seem fair.

Then I had to go to the bathroom.
I took a comic book with me to read.

In no time at all Mom was knocking on the door. "Come out and finish your homework. You've been in there for twenty minutes."

Boy, time sure goes by quick in the bathroom.

Dad came home from work.

It was time for dinner and I was almost finished with my homework.

After dinner my little sister said, "Don't you have to finish your homework?"

She thinks she's so smart 'cause she doesn't have any homework. Just wait and see.

But my homework was gone. I looked everywhere.
I found it all chewed up in the dog's bed.
"What am I gonna do now?" I yelled.

I had to call my best friend and
get all the questions from him.

Mom sat with me to make sure I did my homework. It was real quick to do. Mom looked tired, so I gave her a hug and said . . .

"There, that wasn't so bad, Mom. After all,
it was just a little homework."